The Poison Ivy Case

The Poison Ivy Case

by Joan M. Lexau
pictures by Marylin Hafner

DIAL BOOKS FOR YOUNG READERS
NEW YORK

This special edition for Education Reading Services, Inc.
is published by arrangement with
Dial Books for Young Readers
A Division of E. P. Dutton
A Division of New American Library
2 Park Avenue
New York, New York 10016
Library of Congress Cataloging in Publication Data
Lexau, Joan M. The poison ivy case.
Summary: When Willy gets blamed for his sister's case
of poison ivy, he consults a self-styled witch for help.
[1. Poison ivy—Fiction. 2. Witchcraft—Fiction.]
I. Hafner, Marylin, ill. II. Title.
PZ7.L5895Po 1983 [E] 82-22123
ISBN 0-8037-6910-5 ISBN 0-8037-6924-5 (lib. bdg.)

The art for each picture consists of a pencil drawing
and two pencil overlays reproduced in black, orange,
and blue-green halftone.
Reading Level 2.1

To Marlana Taylor

J.M.L.

To Amanda, Abigail, and Jennifer

M.H.

Willy Nilly's little sister, Tilly,

had an itch.

Oh, what an itch she had!

"Tilly has poison ivy

because of you, Willy,"

said Mr. Nilly.

"Me?" Willy said.

"How did I give her poison ivy?"

His mother said,

"I told you to keep her

in the yard yesterday.

There is no poison ivy there."

Willy yelled, "You think I let her
go out of the yard!
But I didn't!"

"Then how did she catch it?
She was inside with a cold
for a week before that,"
his father said.
Willy didn't know what to say.
How could he make them believe him?

He went out and down the street.

In a store window was a sign.

GOT A PROBLEM?
IF I Can't HeLP you,
No one can.
See the WITCH
in the Orange
House
on GREEN STREET.

"There is no Green Street in town.

The sign must be wrong.

I'll try Orange Street," Willy said.

When he got to Orange Street,

he saw that

all the houses were green.

"I'll try the first house,"

Willy said.

He knocked on the door.

A lady came out.

"Are you a witch?" Willy asked.

BANG!

The lady shut the door in his face.

"Oh, boy!" said Willy.

He walked up and down the street.

There was a broom in one driveway.

Next to the broom

was a big orange cat

with big green eyes.

"HISS!" said the cat.

A sign next to the doorbell said:

MISS HAPP

13 GREEN STREET.

A lady came from the backyard.

She got on the broom

and looked up at the sky.

"Getty up," said the lady.

She jumped as high as she could.

"I did it! I'm flying!" she yelled.

PLOP!

She landed on the cat's tail.

Roowwrrr! the cat yelled

and jumped high in the air.

The lady saw Willy Nilly.

She began to sweep the driveway

very quickly.

"Why are you standing there

spying on people?" she said crossly.

"Are you a witch?" Willy asked.

"Maybe," said the lady.

"I have a problem," Willy said.

"Don't we all," said the lady.

She began to walk away.

She stopped and said,

"Here's my chance.

I could try out my first brew.

Come with me."

They went to her kitchen.

Willy hoped

she knew how to help him.

He told Miss Happ about Tilly

and her poison ivy.

"How can I make my

mother and father believe

that I didn't let Tilly

go out of the yard?" he asked.

Miss Happ took out a blender.

"A pinch of grape seeds," she said.

"And a cup of chunky peanut butter."

She looked around the kitchen.

"Ah. A pint of pancake syrup,"

she said.

She turned on the blender.

"But how will this help?"

Willy asked her.

The witch poured the mix into a jar.

"Take this magic brew and pour it

on your sister's head," she said.

"Huh?" said Willy.

"Now I'm busy," Miss Happ said.
"But come back if you
ever have another problem."
She pushed him out the door.
Willy looked at the magic brew.

"Maybe this will get rid of
Tilly's poison ivy.
Then my parents won't be mad.
That must be
what it's for," he said.
Willy Nilly ran home.

He poured the brew on Tilly's head.

Tilly yelled.

Willy's mother yelled.

His father yelled.

"I know you're mad at us,"
said his mother.
"But don't take it out
on your little sister."
"Just wait," Willy said.
"It will get rid of her poison ivy."
But it did not get rid of
Tilly's poison ivy.
It took Mrs. Nilly two hours
to get the magic brew
out of Tilly's hair.
"No TV for two days, Willy,"
Mr. Nilly said.

Willy went back to see Miss Happ.

He didn't know what else to do.

"You came to thank me.

How nice!" she said.

"The magic brew didn't help,"

said Willy.

24

"Now I can't watch TV for two days.

What should I do?"

"Read a book," said Miss Happ.

"No, about my problem," Willy said.

"What problem?" asked the witch.

"How Tilly got poison ivy

when I didn't let her

go out of the yard," Willy said.

"Why didn't you say so?

I'll need other magic for that.

Show me what you did yesterday

before Tilly got poison ivy,"

Miss Happ said.

The cat jumped on her shoulder.

"Drat will help too," the witch said.

Willy took Miss Happ to his house.

"I came out and sat

on the steps," Willy said.

"Then Mr. Spring from next door

asked me to walk his dog."

"Show me just where you went,"
said Miss Happ.

"Well, okay," Willy said.

"I went around the block."
Willy and the witch
went down the street
and turned the corner.
Willy stopped by an empty lot.

"I let the dog run around in this lot. I stayed here and watched it."

"Did your sister go with the dog?" Miss Happ asked.

"She wasn't with me yet," Willy said. "She didn't come out of the house until I got home with the dog."

"Why didn't you say so!"
said the witch.
"I want to know
what you did when Tilly
was with you."
Just then the wind
blew off a man's hat.

Drat jumped down

and picked up the hat

and ran all over the lot with it.

"Drat you, cat!

Come back here!"

yelled the man.

"That man knows my cat's name!"
said the witch.
"How about that!"
The man looked at Willy Nilly.

"You there, is that your cat?"
he said.
His face was red.

"No," Willy said.

The man looked at Miss Happ.

"Oh, oh!" the witch said to Willy.

"I'm going to make myself invisible."

She waved her arms in the air

and turned around and around,

faster and faster.

She yelled, "Hocus-pocus,

out of focus.

Yah, yah, yah, you can't see me!"

The cat climbed a tree

and dropped the hat

on the man's head.

Miss Happ got dizzy and fell down.

"I could see you all the time,"
Willy said.

"Of course," said the witch.

"I was just invisible to him."

The man was way down the street

running as fast as he could.

"Show me what you did when Tilly

was with you," Miss Happ said.

They went back to Willy's house.

Willy told the witch,

"When I got back with the dog,

Mother told me to stay here

and watch Tilly.

So I did.

Tilly gave the dog a big hug,

and Mr. Spring took it next door.

I told Tilly a long story.

Then we went in to eat."

"Hmm," said Miss Happ.

"So how did Tilly get poison ivy?"

asked Willy.

"I can't tell you right off
the baseball bat," said the witch.
"Drat, do you know?"
Drat scratched her ear
and shook her head.
The witch told Willy,
"I have to work some new spells.
Come see me in the morning."

The next morning Willy Nilly went back to see the witch. She was scratching her arms.

"You!" said Miss Happ.

"Now you've given *me* poison ivy!"

"Oh, no!" said Willy.

The witch said, "I have to know
what spell you used.
Then I can use the right spell
to make it go away."
"But I didn't do it!" Willy yelled.
The witch looked at him
eyeball-to-eyeball.

"Your sister has poison ivy.

I have poison ivy.

But you don't, do you?" she asked.

"No one believes me!" Willy said.

"I'll go to the library.

Maybe they have a book on poison ivy.

I'll find out

what is going on myself."

"Oh! The library!" said Miss Happ.

"No, no, no! Don't do that.

What a silly thing to do.

I have such an itch now,

I can't think.

Come back later.

I'll have your answer then."

Willy went home.

Tilly looked at him and cried.

Willy went out again.

He walked up one street
and down the next.
He went by the library.
On the steps was an orange cat
with big green eyes.
"HISS!" said the cat.
"That must be Drat," said Willy.
He went in the library.

45

Miss Happ was sitting
at a table with a big book.
"Aha!" she yelled.
She snapped the book shut.

"What are you doing here?" she asked.

"I told you not to come."

"What are *you* doing here?"

Willy asked.

The witch said, "I like to come in
on a warm day to get cool."
"But it's cool out today," Willy said.
"So I like to come in
on a cool day to get warm,"
the witch said.

"Now, come with me.

I have a new spell for your problem."

She took him back to the empty lot.

She pointed to it

and shut her eyes and sang,

"Liver, sliver, slimy snoo.

Here's some poison ivy for you."

"Why are we here?" Willy asked.

"I didn't go

in the lot that day.

The dog was in the lot.

And Tilly wasn't with me then."

"Aha!" said the witch.

"The dog was in this poison ivy.

And you said Tilly hugged the dog

when you got home."

"Oh!" Willy said.

"If you touch something
that touched poison ivy,
can you get poison ivy too?"

"Yes," Miss Happ told him.

"I happen to know you can."

She scratched her arms.

"Drat was in that lot too."

"Well, thanks for the magic,"
Willy said.

The witch looked up at the sky.

"I'll work one more magic spell.

I can see Mr. Spring.

Mr. Spring is scratching.

And scratching. And scratching.

And he doesn't know why," she said.

"Oh, no!" Willy said.

"Mr. Spring!"

Willy ran to Mr. Spring's house
and knocked on the door.

Mr. Spring came out.

"I have such a bad case
of poison ivy, Willy," he said.

"I don't know how I got it."

Willy told him how he got it.

Then Willy went home.

He told his mother and father

how Tilly got poison ivy.

Mrs. Nilly said, "We're so sorry

we didn't believe you, Willy."

"Can I watch TV now?"

Willy asked.

"A witch told me to pour

that brew on Tilly's head."

"A witch!" said Mrs. Nilly.

Mr. Nilly laughed.

"Oh, Willy, don't make up stories.

You know we can't believe that!"